Wanted E

By Joanna B

Printed in the United States of America

First Printing, 2014

Pincushion Press

http://pincushionpress.tumblr.com/

Chapters

1

Someone was following her. Again.

It was a perfect day. A warm, early summer day in the middle of June. The sun was shining, the birds were singing.

Kaylie picked up her pace and hurried down the hill toward North Avenue. She had just picked up her diploma and was carrying it home, along with the contents of her locker. Graduation had been a week ago but she'd had to skip it, just like she skipped a lot of things. Sometimes it seemed like all she did was work. School work, homework, house work, work work. She'd been out the last few weeks of high school due to mono but her grades had carried her through. She was an excellent student thank God so her teachers had been lenient.

Mono. What a joke.

They called mono the kissing disease. Like anyone ever kissed her.

It wasn't like she was unattractive. Kaylie knew she was cute. Hot even. With long light brown hair and big brown eyes, and tawny golden skin she knew she had a pretty face. The kind you see in magazines even, with pouty lips and high round cheek bones. Her body was curvy too, despite walking literally everywhere due to a lack of wheels. Her large breasts had made her feel embarrassed when she'd first got them a few years ago. Big and perfectly circular over her absurdly tiny waist and long legs. Her body made her look older in a way that belied her innocence. But she was innocent. Painfully so.

Halfway through her junior year, all the boys in school had abruptly left her alone. They didn't just stop flirting with her or trying to get her to go out with them, they started avoiding her gaze, even pretending that she didn't exist.

It was weird.

Even Janet had said something. Before the sudden change it had been Kaylie who got all the attention from boys. Suddenly it was just the opposite, with her loud mouthed best friend having a date every weekend, not her. Janet was realllllly helpful, just saying that they must have found out about her cooties. Still, they'd both caught the shift, so Kaylie knew she wasn't imagining it.

That was around the same time she'd started noticing the bikes. Wherever she went, whatever time of day, it seemed like there was always a bike behind her. Not just a bike. A *bike.*

It wasn't so crazy to see hogs around. She did live in California. And her town was the epicenter of one of the biggest clubs in the state. But still. It was weird.

She glanced over her shoulder and saw a huge old school motorcycle driving slowlllly up the street behind her. He wasn't looking at her. In fact, he was looking everywhere but at her.

Who knew bikes could even go that slow? And why would he if he wasn't following her.

It was definitely weird.

It had all started when she was serving the counter at Mae's, the diner that everyone still called the soda shop. It had been there since the 1950's, more or less unchanged. She'd worked there since the age of 14 when her mother had insisted she get a job if she wanted to go to college someday. It was out of their reach otherwise, but she'd promised Kaylie would be able to go, no matter what. *If* she worked hard, at school and elsewhere.

Kaylie had taken her mother's advice to heart, and her mother had been true to her word, helping Kaylie save her money for school and making sure the bare necessities were met at home. But it's not like she could afford to buy all the cute outfits that some of the girls at school wore. She had learned to stick to the basics and buy one or two things a year that could go with anything. One pair of jeans, one skirt, one plain blouse, one sweater. That was it. Her wardrobe was not extensive or trendy but it worked as long as she limited the colors she bought. Pink, navy, white, denim. She didn't look frumpy but sometimes she longed to just go to the mall and pick out whatever she wanted. Someday...

It hadn't stopped guys from asking her out in droves though, not until Junior year anyway. She'd just started dating when she could, in between shifts at Maes and working extra hard to make the honor roll. True, she hadn't had a lot of time, but there had been plenty of offers. An absurd amount really. She'd gone out with a few of the boys at school but never let any of them get past first base though. And now, nada.

It's not like she wanted to get pawed in the backseat of a camaro. But it was hard wondering what was wrong with her. Why she was the only girl in school who'd never had a boyfriend... or a prom date. Not that she could have gone to the prom with mono!

She sighed. What was even the point anymore? It's not like any of those high school boys compared to *him*.

Devlin McRae.

It had taken some doing, but she'd found out the name of the guy who'd started coming in almost every time she worked a shift. The guy with the tousled blond hair and green eyes. The guy who looked rough, like he had a past, but who was always polite and left her absurdly large tips.

Everyone seemed to know who he was except her. They all gave him a respectful distance when he came into the diner and sat invariably at the counter, near the end where the waitresses took their breaks between tables.

That was how she ended up spending so much time in his vicinity. Not talking, just... nearby. She tried to ignore the feelings that he created in her, the nervous, jittery tingles, but it didn't really work. She looked forward to seeing him, dreading it at the same time. She was a great waitress when he wasn't in the diner. When else did she drop coffee cups?

She'd decided that if she was going to have a crush, she'd better find out who he was. He rode a bike, she knew that much. He was a little older than her too, in his early or mid twenties. He had a hard look to him but that wavy blond hair was incredibly boyish. Not to mention all those muscles...

No one had wanted to talk about him at first. The name had been hard enough, but finding out that he was the President of the local MC had taken even longer. At 25, he was the youngest President in the history of the club. Devlin was a bad boy for all intents and purposes. Most likely a criminal and definitely the leader of a bunch of criminals and soon to be criminals. Off limits to someone like her certainly.

But dear lord, he was dreamy. As if a model was dressing as a biker for a high fashion photo shoot. He was the real deal though. Dangerous. She could look at him though, right? There was no harm in that... She was subtle about it, just sneaking a peek now and then. That's until she realized *he* was watching *her*.

She'd dropped another coffee cup when she'd caught his eyes on her for the first time. Her whole body had lit up like a christmas tree. He hadn't looked away either. Just sat there, watching her clean up the mess on the floor. When she stood up a few minutes later, he was gone.

And a twenty dollar tip was on the counter.

That was around the time she started noticing the bikes. It never felt threatening. It always felt more like they were escorting her. They didn't stare or cat call. The huge guy with long curly hair nodded at her now and then. That was it. They were just... there.

She turned around and saw the same curly haired guy who was often behind her. He reminded her of a bear, or a villain from an

action movie. The guy looked *intense*. As soon as she turned the
corner to her block though, he was gone. As usual. Well, not gone,
but waiting politely around the corner in case she went out again.
Kaylie lived on a cul de sac so it's not like she could get past him.
Not unless someone hid her in the trunk of their car.

She almost laughed. The whole situation was bizarre. It's not
like she could call the cops or them. 'Um, yeah officer? There's this
guy-well it's not *always* the same guy- but anyway it seems like
there's always a biker half a block behind me. No, they don't
actually *do* anything...'

Yeah, that would go over great.

She wasn't sure she even wanted to call the cops anyway. Not if
the crazy thought she'd been having lately was... true. The crazy
thought she hadn't even admitted to herself or the two girlfriends
who had noticed the bikes. Janet and Lindsey had been freaked out
by it at first but now they didn't even mention it. Just part of the
scenery to them. But Kaylie couldn't stop thinking about the
possibility.

The crazy idea that just felt like it just might be true.

She was starting to believe that they were keeping an eye on her.
Protecting her. For Devlin. It was a crazy thought because he'd
given her no real reason to believe he even knew who she was. He'd
never asked her out or said anything remotely flirtatious to her. He
just placed his order and sat there quietly, eating his food, always
utterly relaxed and confident. He could have owned the place the
way he sat there. He could have owned the world.

But the way he looked at her whenever he came into Mae's... she
caught him watching her hungrily constantly now. He'd stopped
hiding his purpose in being in the diner all together. Eventually
she'd learned not to flinch or drop anything from the incredible
heat coming off the man. He was smoldering. For her.

That much she knew was not her imagination.

Kaylie ran to her house and got dressed for work. She had a shift tonight and as usual, they needed the money. She was attending state school starting in the fall. She could commute from here but ideally she'd be able to get an apartment on her own. Never mind books and bus fare back and forth every day. It was over an hour to campus by public trans. She was not looking forward to that.

Besides, once school started she wouldn't be able to work as many shifts. She'd miss it. Mostly because of Mae of course. But if she was honest with herself she'd also miss bumping into *him*.

I wonder if they'll follow me onto campus?

She giggled at the thought of bikers parked outside her lecture hall and slipped into her pink rayon uniform. Mae's was old school. She didn't mind though. The retro waitress uniform did look pretty cute on her.

2

She poured another cup of coffee for the trucker at the end of the counter. It was already past the end of her shift, nearly 11 o'clock. The whole place would be shut down already if they didn't have one last customer. Charlie, the line cook, was already shut down for the night and only waiting for her out of courtesy. The staff were all very protective of her, especially since she'd started working the late shift.

Kaylie sighed and rested her face in the palm of her hand. It had been an uneventful evening. No sign of *him* tonight. Mae and Sally the afternoon waitress had both left a few hours ago leaving Kaylie with no one to talk to. She'd restocked the entire diner and even read a few chapters of the new book she'd borrowed from the library. But now she was starting to long for bed.

She thought about drinking some coffee herself but she knew she'd be up half the night if she did. She nursed the chocolate milkshake she'd made for herself earlier instead. Everything was already wiped down. She wanted to go home.

Finally the trucker got up and left, putting a few bucks on the counter. Kaylie put the money into the register, pocketed the tip (35 cents) and ran a rag over the spot where the coffee cup had been. Charlie had already put the cup and saucer in the dishwasher so they were out of there in two minutes flat.

She waved goodbye to Charlie and stepped onto the sidewalk, pulling her old wooly cardigan closed in the front to keep warm. It might be June, but it still got cold at night sometimes. It was eerily quiet too, making her look around for her usual motorcycle escort. They were nowhere to be seen at the moment.

She sighed and stepped out onto the sidewalk, turning the corner off the main road.

"Need a ride?"

Kaylie stopped dead in her tracks. Leaning against his bike was a very handsome, very clean shaven, very wrapped in leather and tight jeans Devlin McRae.

Her heart stopped. She stood there dumbfounded before she remembered to take a breath. Inhale. Exhale. In and out. In and out...

Had he been waiting for her?

"Hi."

He grinned and looked up at her from under that lock of blond hair that always seemed to be falling just so over one eye. Her stomach dropped nervously at the come hither look in his green eyes.

Bedroom eyes. So that's what that meant.

He had definitely been waiting for her.

"Hi."

She swallowed nervously, wishing she had drank a cup of coffee after all. Maybe she'd be quick witted instead of standing there like a dullard when the most beautiful, and by far the most dangerous man she'd ever laid eyes on was - what? Asking her out?

No. Not out. He was offering her a ride. That was it. No big deal, right?

It felt like a very big deal. Too big a deal for her to say anything clever certainly.

He didn't seem put off by her silence though. He just held out his hand. There was a helmet in his other hand. For her.

"Don't worry, I'll go slow."

She could have sworn there was something sensual in his smirk as she saw herself putting her hand into his. He wasn't just talking about the bike. He was talking about... other things. She stared up at him as he slid the helmet over her head, locking the chin strap into place. He ran his thumb over her cheek as she blinked up at him, completely under his spell.

Snap out of it girl!

Before she knew it she was behind him, her legs straddling the bike, with her skirt pushed up her thighs. Her arms wrapped tentatively around his taught midriff. Even through the worn leather jacket she could feel his muscles. He had a lot of muscles.

"Hold on."

She tightened her grip as he revved the motor and took off. Her cheek was pressed against his shoulder, and suddenly she could smell him. He smelled like oil, leather and something else she couldn't quite put her finger on. But overall he smelled masculine. Very, very masculine. The rumbling of the bike underneath her felt odd, making her all tingly inside.

Had she been cold before? Because suddenly she was burning up.

****

They rode around the outskirts of town before he headed back toward her house, clearly taking the long way. He pulled over a few blocks from home and turned the bike off. He turned his head and glanced at her over his shoulder.

"Do you need to go right home?"

She shook her head 'no.' Even though she knew her mother would worry if she took too long. Even though she had no idea what Devlin wanted, or anything about him really.

That wasn't exactly true though was it? She did know. She knew he wanted her and she knew he was protective. And tough. But he was always sweet to her. That's all that mattered, right?

Besides, nothing on God's green earth would keep her from going with him tonight. He could have taken her to the moon and she wouldn't have said a peep. The little voice in the back of her head reminded her this was beyond foolish but she ignored it. She knew instinctively that he wouldn't hurt her. Not physically anyway. Protecting her heart was another matter altogether.

He picked up speed as he turned up the mountain road. Recognition set it, along with a renewed feeling of nervousness. He was taking her to the overlook. He must be. That was the only thing up there.

Lovers lane.

Her heart was thudding in her chest as they climbed the sharp curves that led to the infamous make out spot. He took the steep road with ease and confidence. She felt completely safe on the back of his bike. What she was worried about was what would happen when they stopped...

Would he kiss her? Would he want more? It was obvious he liked her. At this point there was no point in lying to herself about that. She liked him too. No, she *wanted* him. She had for a long time.

Now that she had him though, she had no idea what to do with him.

They pulled into the clearing and suddenly the kickstand was down and he was helping her off the bike. There was a knowing look in his eyes when he took off her helmet. He could probably see her blushing! But no- it was dark here. The thought gave her a small measure of comfort. He took her hand and led her over to the rocks overlooking the valley. You could see two counties from up here.

Kaylie watched nervously as he walked unerringly toward a large flat rock and guided her onto it. He sat beside her and stared out at the view. She decided to do the same thing and caught her breath in wonder.

"It's beautiful..."

He looked at her with a hint of surprise.

"You've never been up here before?"

She shook her head shyly.

"No. I mean, not at night."

That made him grin for some reason. Oh. Of course. He could probably tell how ignorant she was about... well everything. She felt ridiculous sitting beside the sexiest man in town like a nun. She realized she was sitting on her hands and yanked them up and into her lap.

He put his arm around her and pulled her against his side. And then... nothing. He just sat there. He was wearing fingerless gloves that scratched her skin when he started to stroke her arm. Her sweater had slid off her shoulder and he was- oh!

Tingles shot through her body from the place where his fingertips brushed her, making lazy circles. With a shock she realized her nipples were getting hard. There was a warm feeling was growing between her legs.

The sensation was unfamiliar to her, strange and exciting. But she knew instinctively what it was. It was desire.

He pulled her in for a kiss, somehow sensing the exact moment that the tides had tipped in his favor. The urge to be close to him was finally overwhelming her nerves. Her lips parted slightly under the pressure of his. He had surprisingly soft lips for a man. Not that she'd ever kissed a man before. A boy, yes. But this was a different matter entirely.

****

Devlin inhaled the scent of the innocent young beauty in his arms. She tasted so sweet, fresh and clean and... chocolatey.

"Hmmmm... you taste good."

He lifted his head to look at her. Her eyes were still closed and a dreamy expression was on her face. He liked it even better than the blush she'd worn when they first arrived. She didn't know it, but he had excellent night vision.

He lowered his head again, before she could come to her senses and wonder why a nice girl like her was kissing the head of the most notorious Motorcycle Club in the county. Hell, the SOS were feared statewide. He grinned and slid his tongue along the soft pink lips, urging her to open her mouth. When she finally did, he eased his tongue inside, twirling it against hers. She let out a startled gasp before settling down again and letting him work his magic on her.

It was clear she hadn't been kissed much. He grinned into her mouth. Instead of turning him off it inflamed him more than he could have imagined. He liked her innocence. He liked it *a lot*.

Of course, he was the one who made it clear to all the young men in town that she was off limits. That was nearly two years ago, and clearly whatever experience she'd had at that point was halted in it's tracks. Once he'd put his claim on her, no one had dared to approach her. He suspected they had barely looked at her in all that time. Safer that way. Better than looking, and wanting... he was the one who'd had to watch her grow up and blossom into the beauty in his arms. He was the one who had been forced to wait.

He pulled her closer, resting his hands firmly on her hips. He resisted the urge to squeeze her round bottom or slide his hand up to her breasts. If she was any of the other women he'd bedded over the years, they'd be undressed and underneath him already. But he'd waited this long for Kaylie, and he could wait a bit longer.

Not *too* much longer though. The bulge in his pants was already becoming uncomfortable. Better to stop for now. They had time. If he had his way about it, she'd be available to him every night from here on out.

Forever.

He gritted his teeth and lifted his head. He'd stopped sleeping with the girls who hung around the club a few weeks ago, knowing that it was almost time to make his move with her. She was the sort of woman that you didn't mind giving up cheap thrills for. Besides, he had a feeling there were plenty of thrills ahead. For both of them.

"I better take you home now. Don't want to worry mama."

****

She nodded, ashamed to admit to herself that she didn't want to leave. Didn't want him to stop kissing her, touching her, maybe even more. She'd forgotten completely about the time. She glanced at her watch and gasped. He was right. Her mom *was* going to be worried. Normally she'd be home by now. No, an hour ago. Dang.

He helped her onto the bike, fixing the helmet into place again. Then he swung on gracefully and kicked the throttle. She wondered how many times he'd done that. Thousands probably. He made it look so easy, like a panther leaping into a tree. Every move he made was clean and spare, without any added flourishes. She rested her cheek against the leather of his jacket, inhaling deeply. Her relief was palpable. He hadn't pushed her to stay out or go further than she wanted to. In fact, if anything, he'd left her wanting more.

They pulled up to her house, making her realize that he knew where she lived. Of course he did. He'd been having her followed, hadn't he? She bit her lip as he lifted her off the bike and undid the strap of her helmet for her. He ran his thumb over her lip this time, his eyes hooded with desire.

She closed her eyes, hoping he would kiss her again.

"Hi Devlin."

Kaylie jumped at her mothers voice but Devlin didn't move. She peeked up at her mother and was surprised to see a placid look on her face as she smiled benignly at the man who'd driven her home on his motorcycle.

"Good evening Mrs. Thomas."

He grinned and winked at Kaylie's shocked expression. He leaned down and placed a soft kiss by her ear.

"You didn't think I was going to take you riding without asking permission did you?"

Her mouth was open as he climbed back on his bike and rode away.

Her mother gestured her inside with a knowing grin.

"What did he-"

"What did he ask me?"

"Yes, and when?"

Her mother grinned and locked the door behind her.

"That's between him and I. Now off to bed. You have a long day tomorrow."

"I do?"

Her mother just smiled and kissed her goodnight.

3

Her mother shook her awake at 8 am. Every fiber of her being longed to stay in bed. She hadn't slept late in so long...

"What is it? Is everything okay?"

"Yes sweetheart. Devlin is picking you up soon."

That got her attention. She sat up.

"He is? What for? *How* soon?"

Her mother shrugged and said "About ten minutes. I'll let him tell you about it. But he said to wear something comfortable and bring a sweater. You'll be out all day."

Kaylie was on her feet in seconds, already in panic mode. Her mother turned back from the hallway before looking over her shoulder coyly.

"Don't forget your bikini."

"WHAT?"

She ran after her laughing mother, swatting her bottom. Why did her mother know more about what her - she didn't know what to call Devlin, not yet anyway - but why did her mother get to know more than *she* did? She grinned suddenly, realizing he must have arranged all of this yesterday or even earlier. Asking her mother for permission was sweet... and unexpectedly old fashioned for a biker.

She felt warm inside at the thought. And if her mother approved... all the better.

It had been just the two of them for so long, ever since her father had passed away. Having someone else besides Mom looking out for her was nice. She was afraid to think about anything past that.

Who knew what his intentions were really? But he was making her wonder if he was after more than just a summer fling. He did seem to be extremely prepared... and determined.

She ran into the bathroom and took the world's fastest shower, giddy with excitement. She slipped into her one bikini and pulled on a pair of cut off jean shorts and a white top with pink flowers covering it. She debated about what to do with her hair and decided to leave it down but to bring a clip so she could pull it back later. It would just get flattened by the helmet anyway. She stuffed a sweater, sunblock and lip gloss into a bag and was chugging a glass of orange juice when she heard the rumble of a bike outside.

He was here.

Devlin rode through the warm June morning toward Kaylie's house. He was pleased, despite everything that had gone down last night. The club was considering taking on new members and had hazed a few promising new prospects from the group that had applied. Things had gotten a little out of hand with one of the young guys and now they had a prospect in the hospital with third degree burns. Dave Fahey had been drinking heavily and dared the foolish kid to shoot flaming liquor out of his mouth. The kid would be alright- he'd even earned the club's respect by not screaming like a woman. But he'd have a pretty big scar and would be forever be known as whisky beard.

Dev hated stuff like that though. It wasn't what the club was about. It was supposed to be a brotherhood of guys with their own code. They had a set of rules and morals that worked, outside and set apart from the rest of society. The average rule following American was a sheep, but the Spawn were the wolves.

Sure, getting hammered was a right of passage for the guys and a way to blow off steam. But not every night. And hurting each other was wasteful- they had enough enemies in the state who were willing to do it for them- on both sides of the law.

He pushed aside the thought of the local law enforcement-Sheriff Dooley in particular had a hard on for Devlin. His second in command Officer Grant was just as bad. He now got facetious parking tickets on a weekly basis. He often found himself with a tail when he was out on his bike. It had forced him to slow down his breakneck pace considerably. But nothing was going to ruin today. He was going to help Kaylie celebrate her graduation and introduce her to the club and their old ladies. Sure it was fast, but he'd been laying the groundwork for years. He'd made his decision. And it was obvious to him that Kaylie was on board with it.

He grinned, imagining her wearing his jacket- and nothing else. Her hot little body had felt so good pressed against him last night-all warmth and sweet innocence. Well, for now anyway. He didn't bother pretending he'd let her stay innocent for long. He wasn't a man used to denying himself. Definitely not when it came to women.

This wasn't going to be easy.

Then again, nothing worth doing ever was.

He pulled up to her house and parked his bike. Before he could even climb out she was coming out the door looking like sunshine and promises. He felt an odd feeling in the pit of his stomach as she came toward him in a pair of cut off jean shorts and a pretty floral blouse. When she got closer he saw the strap of a bikini top peeking out from around her neck. It was yellow and white gingham.

Damn but she looked fine!

He had the sudden feeling that he might be the one who was out of his depth, not the innocent 18 year old virgin walking toward him. She moved so gracefully, her sweet little body swaying in an unconsciously seductive way. He swallowed, his mouth feeling dry.

She stared up at him trustingly with her big brown eyes while he fitted her helmet over her soft golden brown waves. He couldn't help but brush his hand over the softness of her cheek before helping her onto the bike and climbing on in front of her. He lifted his hand, waving to the woman watching them from the stoop. She waved back with a stoic expression on her face.

It was a good thing he'd been working on Mrs. Thomas for a few years now. He'd made sure the woman hadn't lifted a bag of groceries from the first day he'd noticed Kaylie. She was a smart woman. She knew it wasn't a bad thing to be connected to the club in this town. She'd never have to deal with a flat tire, or a bothersome neighbor. They'd take care of everything for her.

He grinned to himself as he pulled away from the curb. Kaylie arms snaked around toward his stomach sending a jolt of arousal straight through him. It wasn't a bad exchange at all.

4

He hadn't told her where they were going and she hadn't asked. It only occurred to her how odd that was after they'd been riding for a half an hour. She'd been too absorbed by the sensation of the bike, the scenery, and him. Most of all him.

It didn't really matter anyway. If he wanted to surprise her, she'd let him. Even if she wanted to ask him, it would have to wait until he pulled over. There was no way he would hear her over the rumble of the bike.

It was the sort of thing that should make her hate traveling this way. Clinging to him, with zero control over where they were going, how far or how fast. But she didn't hate it at all.

She loved it.

It surprised her how much she loved it. The speed, the smell, the incredible riskiness of it all. But most of all, she loved that she wasn't riding alone. They were together. Fused into one. She trusted him implicitly. Maybe it was foolish, but it was true.

They'd left town far behind already and were heading through endless fields of corn and other crops. She felt her curiosity rise again. There was nothing out this way, unless he planned on taking her over the state line. What was he up to?

It was another ten minutes or so before she realized where they were going. The lake. The County Fair. Child like excitement flowed through her. If she could have jumped up and down, she would have.

It had been years since she'd been to the County Fair. It was easily an hour away and her mother didn't have the time or money to travel for frivolous reasons. Kaylie had always loved the little day trips they'd taken as a family, when her father was still alive. It had been a yearly event for them. After he passed though, the trips had stopped. A lot of things had stopped.

She didn't blame her mom though. Raising a child alone was difficult, and she didn't have an extended family to help out. They'd had family time in other ways. Mostly the sort that involves hard work and chores. Every Sunday after church they spent a few hours cutting coupons. It was fun. Well, kind of.

Kaylie's mother wasn't the sort to kick up her heels or laugh at something just for the fun of it. That had been Kaylie's dad. The joker, the prankster, the life of the party. She missed him each and every day. Her mom did too. It was obvious what she was thinking about when Kaylie caught her gazing out the window or just staring into space. She did that a lot.

Dad had been the one who came up with the fun things to do. He always had a plan or a game to play. But he could be serious too, like about making sure Kaylie knew that she had self worth. He'd instilled that in her early.

'Don't be a pushover Kaylie. Stand up for yourself.'

She'd listened to him when he said that. She'd heard.

She was still thinking about her father when they pulled up to the camp grounds next to the fair. Devlin parked the bike near a row of Harley Davidsons. A bunch of people waved at him but he just nodded and helped her with her helmet.

"Are you hungry?"

She shook her head.

"Thirsty?"

She shook her head again.

"Do you need to use the facilities?"

"No, thank you."

He grinned as if that were the cutest thing he had ever heard. For some reason, it annoyed her that this big tough man was treating her like a puppy. A desirable puppy, but a pet all the same. She frowned at him.

"What's so funny?"

"So polite. It's adorable."

Her cheeks got warm as he leaned down to kiss her. It was only their second kiss and this time it was in broad daylight. She sighed as his lips pressed into hers. His arms slid around her waist to her lower back. His hands were warm and-

"Dev! I hope you're hungry! We're grilling already man!"

Devlin lifted his head with an exaggerated sigh. Kaylie giggled at the look on his face. He threw his arm over her shoulder and walked toward the group of bikers. One of them, a biker with flaming red hair, let out a low whistle at the sight of Kaylie.

"Is she new? Man, put me on the list for some of that."

One of the other bikers, the other one with spiky black hair who often trailed her, elbowed him in the side. Hard. It looked like it hurt. Devlin walked past them, ignoring them completely.

"Ow man, what the fuck? I was just saying I'd be down for sloppy seconds."

"Not this one. Just shut up."

Kaylie wasn't sure what she'd just overheard. Devlin didn't seem too concerned as they walked down a short slope to a flat barbecue area near the lake with about twenty picnic tables. It was meant for families most likely but the entire area was completely over run with bikers. Then again, Kaylie saw a few kids running around here and there. Bikers had families too.

She grinned a little bit at the incongruous sight of a huge tattooed man in leather lifting a little girl in a ballerina costume onto his shoulders. As soon as the man saw Devlin and her, he walked over. In fact, it seemed like everyone started to come over. They were swarmed in minutes as people approached to give Devlin their respects.

"This must be Kaylie. I'm Bob and this is Sally. Congrats on graduating, honey."

The big man held out a beefy hand. Kaylie shook it shyly before reaching up and shaking the adorable little girls hand, making her giggle.

He'd told them about her. When?

People waited politely to meet her and to bring Devlin and her drinks and food. She sipped a cold beer as she watched the bikers pull glass beer bottles from a row of stocked coolers. Coolers that sat right underneath a sign that said 'no glass containers.'

She had to laugh. The MC certainly did not follow the rules. But they did come up and introduce themselves, one by one. She finally met the big biker with long curly hair, Jack. He was Devlin's second in command. Then there was Donahue with merry blue eyes and black spiky hair, always hovering somewhere near Jack or Dav. She met Mike, also known as Whisky beard, one of the young prospects who she recognized from high school who had an angry red splotch on his cheek. There were too many other names to remember them all. She hoped she'd get the hang of it eventually.

Eventually. Everything about this felt like he was interested in being her boyfriend. Did bikers even date? She decided not to worry about it. Not yet.

In the midst of the introductions Kaylie noticed that at least a few people were less than enthusiastic about Devlin's arrival with her. The red haired biker seemed to be annoyed about the scenario. But it wasn't him that set off alarm bells in Kaylie's head.

Two women stood off to the side. Both were blond and attractive. One of the women was in her 30's but the other one looked only a couple of years older than Kaylie. Long blond hair, peachy skin, and a body that looked like she could moonlight as a swimsuit model. She would have been stunning if not for the pinched look on her face. For a moment Kaylie wondered what was wrong with her. Until she realized what is was. A heavy feeling settled in the pit of her stomach.

Oh. She was jealous.

Kaylie wondered if the girl had been Devlin's girlfriend before her. Maybe he ran through girls like tissue paper. Maybe she was being taken advantage of. She felt herself getting quiet, letting the conversations around her wash over her like water.

"Let's take a walk."

She looked up at him and nodded. Devlin pulled her out of the crowd to a path that circled the lake.

"Okay Kaylie, what's bothering you?"

He didn't sound mad, she realized thankfully. But he was throwing her off balance. He really did not beat around the bush did he? Well, then she wouldn't either.

"I'm not sure what I'm doing here."

"You're going for a walk. After that you are going to a picnic and after that, you are going to a carnival."

She stopped walking and gave him an exasperated look. He just grinned at her. The man was far too pleased with himself.

"Yes, but why?"

"Because you graduated."

"But why am I here *with you?*"

He gave her a knowing look and leaned back against a tree, crossing his arms.

"Don't tell me you don't know."

"I'm not being coy Devlin. I know you like me. I just don't know how many other girls get the royal treatment. There was a blond back there giving me evil looks. I don't want to step on someone else's territory."

He laughed.

"You are definitely not coy. Yes, I like you. No, there aren't any other girls. And no one has ever gotten the royal treatment before you. *Ever.*"

She narrowed her eyes at him, undecided.

"Come here, Kaylie."

She stayed where she was, lifting her chin. He laughed again and was on her in a second, lifting her up and over his shoulder like she weighed less than a rag doll. He carried her back to the tree and leaned her against the rough bark. Then he leaned over her, boxing her in with his arms.

Her breath was coming fast and shallow as he leaned forward with a heavy lidded look in his eyes. She looked away, suddenly nervous. He lifted her chin with one hand, forcing her to meet his eyes. What she saw there took her breath away. He wanted her. Even more than she realized. It was written all over his face.

"I know what I want and I go after it. I don't lie and I don't cheat. I'll take care of you if you let me Kaylie."

Her mouth opened slightly at his proclamation.

"Are you asking me to be your girlfriend?"

He just grinned and leaned forward, his mouth less than an inch from her ear.

"I'm asking for a little more than that. I play for keeps."

"Oh."

Her whole body was tingling from his nearness. She was trembling a little bit she realized. She hoped he didn't notice. He kissed her ear and then moved below it, nuzzling her neck deliciously with his soft lips.

"So?"

"What?"

Her voice sounded breathy, a ridiculous caricature of a woman in the throws of lust. He kept kissing her neck, working back up to her ear.

"Is the answer yes?"

She could barely think but she managed to get out a shaky nod and a whispered yes. He was staring down at her with a triumphant look on his face.

"Good. Because I wouldn't have left you alone anyway."

She should have been annoyed at his cockiness but she wasn't. Instead it sounded like an oath of something. Something deep and true.

They both moaned as their lips met. He was finally kissing her, their breath commingling as they grasped each other desperately. He lifted her slightly, pushing her back into the tree trunk and pressing his body against hers. She gasped at the feeling of his hardness pressing into her belly. Oh god, he wanted to...

He was laughing again as he pulled away, stroking her hair gently. He lifted his body away from the intimate position they'd been in. She sighed as he broke contact, wanting him back against her almost immediately.

"No Kaylie I'm not going to try to do *that* in a public park."

"I knew that."

"Did you?"

She just stared at him, hoping her breath would return to normal, hoping she'd get used to the whirlwind of emotions he created in her so easily. It was annoying, how easy it was for him to turn her upside down. She decided it was important for her peace of mind that he didn't know the full extent of the control he had over her body and senses.

Because if he knew, who knew what he would do?

5

Devlin stared down at Kaylie. He was sorely tempted to find a private place to continue what they'd started but he put it out of his mind. He knew he wouldn't go through with it anyway. Kaylie was not the sort of girl you took in a parking lot. She still looked concerned, even though he'd kissed her senseless less than a minute before.

"Any other questions for me sweetheart?"

"Yes. I mean, just one."

"Go ahead."

"Why me? It can't just be my-"

He grinned and raised an eyebrow.

"Your charms?"

She nodded sheepishly. Her charms were exceptional and certainly part of the reason he'd been drawn to her. But that wasn't why he'd first noticed her. In fact, he had started going to the diner because of Johnny.

"That's part of it. You are incredibly beautiful Kaylie."

She looked doubtful at that. He tried not to laugh again. His girl was sheer perfection. Beautiful but not vain, naturally sexy without any artifice or vulgarity. She deserved a real answer though, not flattery. He took a deep breath, hoping she wouldn't take this the wrong way.

"It started with Johnny."

"Johnny? The little boy who-"

He nodded. Johnny was mentally disabled. Sweet kid, industrious, even had a paper route. But he was special, and he'd had a hard time of it with the other kids making fun of him. The trouble was, he was just smart enough to *know* he was different. That was the hardest part.

"Johnny was always talking about this pretty girl who gave him an extra scoop of ice cream at Mae's. The kid loved going to that place. He even got a second job mowing lawns so he could afford to go in twice a week."

"He was a sweet boy. All I did was talk to him."

"It meant a lot to him Kaylie. So after he died I went in there to have his favorite. In his honor."

She smiled sadly.

"Banana split with extra nuts."

"Right. And then this stunningly beautiful girl walks over and takes my order. I couldn't believe there was an angel like you in this town. I knew I had to make you mine."

"Me? You are joking right?"

"Do I seem like I'm joking?"

She stared up at him and he raised his eyebrow as he smiled at her. She blushed immediately which made him smile even wider.

"Unfortunately, you were a little too young for me. So I had to wait."

"I still don't understand. Did Johnny come around the clubhouse or something?"

"Yeah, he hung out there a lot. Johnny was my brother."

Her sweet little mouth dropped open and a look of concern replaced the disbelief that had been there a moment before.

"I'm so sorry Devlin. I didn't know. We were all so sad about what happened to him. Oh god-"

She stared at him, finally putting the pieces together. Johnny and his mother had died in a car accident. That meant...

"You lost your mother too... Oh god, I'm so sorry."

He smiled at her softly. He really appreciated her words of condolence. They meant something.

"Thank you."

"So that's why you came in every week?"

"I had to check up on you and see how you were doing. I kept hoping you'd give me an extra scoop of ice cream but you never did."

He looked so sad for a minute that she laughed. A serious look came over her face. It looked like the disbelief was back.

"You've been waiting this whole time? That was almost two years ago!"

He shook his head. He wasn't going to lie to her. She didn't need to know how many girls he'd had, or how many offers he'd turned down, including a couple of girls who'd wanted to fool around last night at the clubhouse after he'd dropped her off.

"I'm not a monk Kaylie. But I will be true to you."

She looked thoughtful for a minute. So she wasn't going to raise a fuss about all the other women. And there had been a lot. That was a relief. There was no way to explain that away, even to an innocent like Kaylie.

"Okay. I will be true too."

He laughed and she slapped his shoulder.

"What's so funny?"

"Nobody would try it sweetheart, no matter how much they wanted to."

She blushed, clearly understanding what he was saying to her. Nobody messed with Devlin or his riders.

"Come on, let's get something to eat."

6

Kaylie licked the hot sauce off her fingers and leaned back on the blanket that had magically appeared for them. So had two full plates of food along with two frosty cold beer bottles. She was already getting used to that. All the little things the people in the club did for Devlin. It wasn't just the club members, it was the prospects, the girlfriends, the hanger ons. Even the older generations were represented and went out of their way for Devlin. It really was a family picnic. And they all looked up to *him*.

Devlin was beside her, nursing his beer. He had been sipping the same bottle for at least an hour. She knew it was for her benefit. He wouldn't drink and drive with her on the back of his bike.

Things were definitely going better since their talk. Kaylie was finally relaxing and just enjoying herself. She hadn't seen the blond girl anywhere either. Maybe she had been imagining the girl's animosity. She was probably just a hanger on after all. There were a lot of sexy looking girls hanging around who didn't seem attached to anyone. A few were oiling themselves up and laying out in the sun to tan, but it was obviously just a ploy to get one of the guys to notice them. It probably worked. They were putting on quite a display. Devlin never once looked over there though. He was a gentleman through and through underneath all that leather.

Kaylie smiled to herself, wondering how Devlin would react to seeing her in her bikini. It was a little small on her truth be told. After all, the last time she'd had need of a bikini she'd been 15 years old and working at a summer camp during the day. She had definitely filled in since then. A lot.

But the lake looked inviting on such a warm day. It had been ages since she'd gone swimming. Besides, it would be extremely interesting to see if Devlin liked what he saw... She decided that she might as well go for it before she lost her nerve. She pulled her top off over her head in a fluid motion and got to her feet.

"What are you-"

"Swimming silly. Don't you want to come?"

She shimmied her cut off shorts down over her hips and smiled over her shoulder at him. The poor man looked thunderstruck as she laughed and ran towards the water. She'd never seen him looking anything but self assured. She doubted anyone ever had. He was the one sitting on the throne after all. He'd been born and bred to lead. He'd been the President since coming of age five years ago. Everyone knew that.

She ran into the water and dove in, ignoring the hooting and hollering all around her. The crowd of bikers had gone crazy as she dashed toward the sand, turning her cheeks bright pink. She came up gasping for air from the sudden chill. The water was way colder than she'd expected it to be! All the sudden she felt arms close around her and turned, sputtering with indignation.

Devlin smiled down at her, his wet hair curling over his forehead.

"You didn't think I was going to let you go in by yourself looking like that did you?"

She smiled at him.

"A lot of the girls are wearing bikinis."

He smiled and lifted her up before tossing her into the water a few feet away. She grabbed his ankle playfully under the water until he yanked her up into his arms again.

"Yeah but not one of them looks even remotely like you do. Jesus woman!"

"You're the one who told me to wear a bikini."

"I'm a genius."

"Well, you are smarter than you look..."

He growled at her as she pushed off and swam deeper from the shore. They didn't notice the eyes watching them from across the lake.

****

Dani was pouting as she watching Devlin and his new tramp frollicking in the water. He'd never acted that way with her. All he'd done was crook his finger when he wanted to fool around and pretty much ignored her the rest of the time.

But oh my, he'd been amazing in bed. She'd had plenty of guys before and since of course. None had come even close to matching Dev. Damn him and his sudden interest in relationships.

She'd known this was coming of course. Everyone had known that Devlin had a special lady in mind and was waiting until she was of age. But she hadn't imagined the hot slice of jealousy that would rip through her guts at the sight of them together.

Why hadn't he been that way with *her?*

"What'd you want to see me about Dani?"

She turned at the sound of Officer Grant's gravelly voice behind her. She flared her eyes at him coquettishly and he narrowed his, looking her over.

He'd asked her out before so she knew he liked what he saw. So far she had yet to give into his attentions.

"You're always saying how you wanted to put him away. Well, so do I."

"Oh really? How the tides have turned."

"Office Grant I have *always* been on the right side of the law!"

He grinned and stepped forward, grabbing her hips.

"I'd rather have you under it."

She giggled nervously. He was a little bit too aggressive for her taste. But if she had to give in to get what she wanted, so be it.

"That can be arranged."

He grunted and kissed her mouth hard. Then he lifted his head up and looked around making sure nobody could see them. He grabbed her hand and yanked her back towards a copse of trees and bushes.

Oh crap.

Dani's plan was to cause Devlin and his new hussy some trouble. Not to get mauled by Officer Friendly in the bushes. The last thing she needed was to get poison ivy on her ass.

"Um... Grant? What is your plan exactly?"

He turned once they were screened from the rest of the camp grounds and grinned at her, reaching for his belt buckle.

"I thought we'd kill two birds with one stone."

"Two birds?"

He nodded, his hands moving to his shirt buttons. Once they were undone, he reached for her.

"Uh huh. One bird is getting me laid. The other bird is getting Dev thrown in jail. And you're going to help me with that. Don't scream if I get a little rough. It's just for effect. Your job is make sure someone sees you guys together later tonight."

Her eyes widened as she took in his meaning. He ripped her shirt off, scratching her skin. Dani had to bite her lip to keep from whimpering as he forced her onto the ground.

7

Devlin was letting himself be led around the State Fair like a dog on a leash, but he didn't care. Kaylie's enthusiasm for the carnival was contagious. He realized he'd been smiling non stop while his woman dragged him onto various rides and fed him little bits of cotton candy.

Until he'd noticed her. The girl with long blond hair was following them.

Dani.

A couple of years ago he'd had a thing with Dani. Nothing serious, just fooled around a couple of times. She was a good looking girl but her attitude was always out of control and her mood swings made her not a lot of fun to be around. She was the younger sister of one of the club's old lady's so he couldn't just ignore her until she went away when he was done with her like he usually did with women. He'd had to sit down and have a talk with her about why it wasn't going to work out.

Hell, they'd just been kids. It was never going to 'work out' for them anyway. But Dani hadn't taken it well. And she hadn't given up hope. He'd never had a girlfriend in all the time since. Lots of girls had helped him pass the time but never for long. She hadn't much liked any of those girls either.

But this was different. He wouldn't let her intimidate his woman, or ruin even a second of her celebration today. Kaylie had already mentioned a blond girl staring at her. It would not make her happy if she found out Dani was his ex, or that she'd been trailing them all night. He would do anything to protect Kaylie, even if he had to tell Dani to back off and risk offending Bruce and his old lady Janine.

It didn't make sense though. Dani had to have known about Kaylie for a while now, everyone in the club did. He'd been having the guys look after her for so long now, it was hardly a secret what his intentions were. So acting surprised and jealous seemed way out of line. But there Dani was, stalking them like a jealous exgirlfriend. Which she hadn't been. Not really. He frowned as he followed Kaylie into the fun house, catching a flash of blond hair behind them. He could tell she'd been crying.

Damn it.

Thankfully Jack and Donahue were with them at the moment. He jerked his head backwards and whispered.

"Get rid of her."

Jack was gone in an instant, leaving Donahue to trail them through the fun house. Kaylie was laughing as a clown jumped out at them. He slipped his arm around her and used the scare as an opportunity to kiss her neck.

Hmmmm... he was going to have a hard time waiting to take her. Even if he knew he'd have her in his bed within the hour, it would be a painful wait. But he had promised himself (and her mother in less explicit terms) that he wouldn't take her for at least a week. She deserved that at the very least. She was a complete innocent as far as he could tell. He had to make sure that she was sure before he convinced her to lay down with him. That part would be easy. Getting his body to hold off for release was something else entirely.

He could ease into it though, take things a bit farther every night. He grinned at the thought, planning explicitly what he would do each night, and where. Only five more nights to go.

****

Kaylie inhaled as Devlin's hand closed over her breast. They were on the swing in the playground across the street from her house, hidden from view from the high fence. They'd been kissing for a half hour at least when he started sliding his hands over her body, getting more and more intimate with each pass.

She was surprisingly relaxed about kissing Devlin. He still made her head spin, but she wasn't terrified of doing it wrong, like she had been the first few times. She swirled her tongue against his playfully, eliciting a low growl from his throat. She was starting to get used to his sounds. He made the sexiest little noises when he was kissing her. And now that his hands were wandering his breathing was getting raspy.

His hand disappeared and a finger replaced it, tracing the outline of her nipple which was poking through her bikini and thin cotton top. Her sweater must have fallen off... or more likely, he had pushed it off to get better access to her. A strange feeling was coursing through her body, centering in between her legs. This was more intense than the other times. He wasn't being playful now. He was serious.

She gasped as he pinched her nipple lightly. He laughed throatily, resting his forehead on hers.

"Oh so you like that do you?"

She didn't trust herself to speak while he traced the collar of her blouse, dipping his finger inside to pull on her bikini strap. His other hand reached around her and pulled her tightly against him. Against the burning heat of his erection.

Oh god...

He pulled her top down and to the side, then pushed the triangle of her bikini top covering her breast aside. Suddenly she was completely bare to him. He moaned and lowered his head to her chest, suckling her nipple lightly.

She felt herself slipping backwards in his embrace as her hands wound through his hair, clasping his head closer to her. He moaned and rocked his hips gently into hers rhythmically. He pulled her top down on the other side and started kissing her other breast. Now he was alternating back and forth, using his hands and tongue to tweak her nipples, driving her insane with desire.

They were both making soft guttural sounds as he guided her legs around his waist, bringing her feminity into direct contact with... him. They were practically lying down on the swing she realized. It was a good thing it was dark out!

"Damn... we better stop."

Kaylie felt dazed as he pulled her into a sitting position and adjusted her top back into place. He was breathing heavily and looked strange. As if he was concentrating on something. Or in pain.

"Are you alright?"

"Yeah, I'm- Don't look at me like that Kaylie. Please... oh god."

He pulled her back into his arms and kissed her deeply. She forgot everything for a moment. Who she was, where she was, who he was to her... If he had wanted to take her then and there, she would have let him.

He let out a muffled curse as he forcefully lifted her to her feet, placing her at arms length from his body. She chewed her lip and stepped toward him.

He laughed harshly.

"Sweetheart, trust me, you do not want to get close to me right now."

"Why not?"

He gave her a wry smile, before his eyes shifted to her heaving bosom. He closed his eyes and held her shoulders so she wouldn't come any closer.

"Because that's not how this is going to happen."

"What?"

"Your first time."

"Oh."

He had a sudden thought and looked at her almost hopefully.

"It will be your first time, won't it Kaylie? Because if not..."

She was tempted to lie to him if it would get him to kiss her again. But she wouldn't do that. Besides, he'd find out soon enough. She felt her cheeks turning pink at the thought. She wanted him to take her. She wanted him.

Badly.

"I'm sorry... I've never... been with anyone else."

He just stared at her, the look in his eyes making her shiver.

"Did I do something wrong? Maybe you don't want to be with someone as inexperienced as me."

He groaned and pulled her into his arms, kissing her hungrily. Then he pushed her away again.

"No Kaylie. Trust me, that's not a problem. You are perfect."

She smiled up at him, feeling reassured. She took another step in, hoping he'd kiss her like that again. He laughed and gave her a gentle little shove, pushing her toward the street.

"And now you better take that sweet perfection inside."

She pouted and looked over her shoulder at him. He just stared at her.

"Go on."

"Goodnight Devlin."

"Goodnight Kaylie."

8

He saw her every night that week, even on the nights she worked at Mae's. He'd come in for a banana split, just like Johnny used to like. She made sure to give him an extra scoop as a sign of her affection, which made him grin. It was always toward the end of her shift when he'd come strolling into Mae's, looking like a hawk in a dovecote. Then he'd wait at the counter until she was ready to go home. They would find a quiet spot to talk and fool around for a couple of hours. Her mother was always up reading when she got home, with no recriminations. Even she trusted Dev with her daughter. If only she knew that it was Kaylie who was starting to get impatient. She wanted the real thing.

She was ready.

When she said goodnight to him on Thursday he was quiet, grim even. They'd gone further than ever before. She'd even touched him there- through his pants. He'd felt so big and warm- dangerously powerful but also- so tempting and exciting. She kissed his cheek while he stared at her darkly, biking off as soon as the front door was closed, without the final wave that he usually gave her.

Little did she know, that was the last she would see of him for 48 hours. He didn't visit her the next night at Mae's during her shift, or call. There was a bike parked outside the whole night though she knew it wasn't his. She was already learning to recognize which ride belonged to who. When she finally closed up it was Jack who followed her home. He didn't offer her a ride or an explanation. As usual, all he did was nod.

Kaylie wasn't sure why Devlin was staying away from her, but she felt awful about it. Her insides felt like they were hollow, empty. Maybe she should have let him do more. He hadn't pushed her but maybe she had missed a cue from lack of experience. He must be bored with a virgin. Maybe he didn't want her anymore...

She cried into her pillow for hours, tossing and turning. She made sure her light was out so when her mother came in to say goodnight, she wouldn't notice her red eyes or tear stained cheeks. It was near dawn by the time Kaylie fell into a fitful sleep.

It was the longest night of her life.

Devlin was in hell. It was ironic that someone with the nickname of 'Devil' would end up in hell. Even more surprising was that he was loving every minute of it. Well, not every minute. Not the past two days.

Kaylie was driving him insane. He'd seen her every night this week and every night he'd dared to go a little further with her. But once he'd opened pandora's box, she was the one who didn't want to stop. He grimaced, just thinking about what she'd done to him two nights ago... once again leaving him with an uncomfortable erection.

He'd even stayed away last night to see if he could loosen her hold on him. He was the one who'd drank beer after beer, staring miserably at the clock, counting the hours until he could see her again. It was happening so fast- this feeling that he wasn't just him anymore- now he was part of an 'us.' It wasn't even just wanting her, thought that was a big part of it. He didn't feel like he was in control of his feelings anymore. He didn't like it.

Two nights ago they'd been fooling around for an hour, he'd finally touched her between her legs, over her tight denim shorts. He'd been wondering about the wisdom of unzipping her shorts when he'd felt her tentative caress on the front of his jeans. Jesus. That fluttering little touch had almost sent him over the edge. And then she'd gotten bolder.

He'd had to take another cold shower last night. He was enjoying her, more than he thought was possible, but his patience was wearing thin.

Tonight was the night. He was done waiting, and if he were honest with himself, she seemed to be done waiting too. If he could just get through this meeting he'd be fine. He was finding him mind was less focused than usual. He forced himself to listen careful to what Jack was reporting. The new Sheriff was making things difficult for the club. They already knew that. But now it was looking like his animosity was specifically targeted at Devlin.

He'd been ticketed again last night, after he'd dropped off Kaylie thankfully. He didn't want to think about giving the cops a chance to hassle his woman. She was so delicate... he frowned at the thought of upsetting her. Enough was enough.

"This stops now. Find out what they have on me. You still in with your cousin, Donnie?"

Donahue nodded. His cousin was on the force one town over. He couldn't keep the cops off their asses but he could tip them off when a big bust was brewing. The Spawns of Satan, also known as the SOS, didn't officially traffic in drugs, guns or hookers, but they did have their own set of laws. And they did *partake* in drugs, guns and hookers. Well not Dev, but a lot of the guys did. He didn't enjoy drugs because of his need for control and he never needed to pay for sex. In fact, he spent most of his time turning women down.

It was a running joke at the clubhouse that Dev had the best sloppy seconds. Girls just hung around waiting for him to notice them all the time. If he did, he didn't usually see them more than once. When he passed them over, they became easy pickings for the rest of the guys in the club. He couldn't tell you the number of times he'd been credited with getting another Spawn laid. For the most part, Devlin ignored it. Sex was just sex. He saw no need to talk about it.

Being good looking was definitely part of it, but it was the power of running the SOS that had made it go over the top. He was bored by it. He knew what he wanted and he'd found it. His mind wandered back to Kaylie and what they'd be doing later tonight. He couldn't wait to make her his once and for all.

He had to take care of this cop situation so it didn't blow back on her. Once people knew she was his old lady, she'd be affected by everything he did. Speaking of which, Jack hadn't had an easy time getting rid of Dani the other night at the State Fair. She'd resisted his guttural demand to vacate the carnival apparently. He'd had to use some rough moves on her to get her to leave. He hadn't hurt her, Dev wouldn't stand for that, but it hadn't been pretty. Dev was pretty sure they should expect more trouble from Dani, brother in law in the Club or not.

"Okay find out what's up. And get Bruce in here. I need to talk to him about his sister in law."

"Dani?"

"Yeah."

He drummed his fingers on the heavy wood table. The meeting room was large enough to accommodate the core members of the club, but they were growing. They also had a couple of other smaller clubs that were part of a larger circle, counting themselves as unofficial members of the SOS. Kind of like cousins.

Things were changing. Someone had even mentioned changing the name of the Club from Spawns of Satan to Devil's Riders. He didn't mind being called Devil but naming the club after him seemed like a slap in the face to the old timers. To his own father and grandfather who'd started the club. He could picture them rolling over in their graves at the thought. Devil's Riders was fine as a nickname but that was it. Still, he couldn't help but notice how many people had started using it.

Bruce walked in and sat down at the table with Dev and Jack. Donnie shut the heavy wood door and leaned against it. Devlin stared at Bruce for a couple of minutes before starting. The older club member looked nervous which was pretty funny considering the guy was a 6'4" wall of muscle and had been in and out prison most of his adult life. He'd calmed down in his mid thirties after getting hitched and was spending less and less time at the clubhouse these days. It was a good thing he'd been there tonight or they would have had to call him in. Who knows how long that would have taken.

"Thanks for coming Bruce. I need to talk to you about your sister in law."

Bruce nodded.

"Dani's been out of control lately. I heard about what happened at the carnival, man. I'm sorry."

"Can you get her to chill out?"

He shook his head.

"I haven't seen her all week, man. I can definitely try but the problem's not just her. It's my old lady too. They are both in a tizzy about your new girl. Calling her an interloper. Saying she's friends with cops."

"She went to high school with a few of the newer cops but that's it. Hell, she went to school with whisky beard too. It doesn't matter anyway. Kaylie is my old lady now. She's off limits to this kind of bullshit."

"Congrats Dev. I didn't know that."

Dev nodded.

"Okay, you need to get your old lady in line. I won't tell you how to do it. Rip up her credit cards or something. If she or Dani come near Kaylie again they will be banned from the club house. Permanently."

Bruce inhaled sharply but nodded. He knew the drill. Dev put Dani and the club out of his mind as the older man left. He was grinning when Donnie handed him a beer.

"No thanks man. I have a date tonight."

Donnie rolled his eyes at him.

"Yeah, we know."

"Did you get the cabin aired out?"

"Yeah, man it's full of fucking rose petals too."

"Very funny. See you tomorrow my brothers."

He clasped their hands and strode out of the club house. It was time to go and get his woman.

9

Kaylie knew something was up. Devlin had shown up tonight as if nothing had happened between them. He seemed tense, and offered no explanation for staying away the night before. She decided not to ask, knowing that if he was here now, whatever was bothering him had nothing to do with her, or he'd resolved it on his own.

It might have only been a week that they'd spent together, but she'd been observing him covertly for the past few years. At least when he came into the diner anyway. Apparently, he'd been observing her too. Everywhere. She knew he was fiercely independent and tended to do things on his own, though always with the club at his back. She was already attuned to his mood shifts. He wasn't a talker, or morose, but he his emotions ran deep, particularly where she was concerned.

He was definitely still worried about something, she could tell. It was obvious from the moment he arrived to pick her up. She hurried out to the bike and slid her arms around his neck. He smiled and kissed her before pulling her onto the bike. He was in a hurry to leave.

They were off and running the moment she had her arms around his waist. As usual he didn't tell her where they were going. And as usual, she didn't mind. Judging from this week, she'd been taken to scenic spots and a few bar-b-q's, even one home cooked meal at his Aunt Edna's house. His folks were gone so she knew it was the equivalent of meeting the parents.

Things were moving fast. Really fast. Kaylie was surprised that she didn't mind. In fact, she wanted to go faster.

Dating a biker was bringing out all sorts of surprising personality traits in her.

No, they weren't dating. It was more than that. They'd skipped all the courtship, although she supposed he'd been courting in his own way by looking out for her and coming into Mae's all those years.

They weren't dating. They were *together*.

The thought sent a warm feeling shooting through her insides. She knew she was in danger of falling in love. It wasn't that she didn't trust him. She did, she trusted him implicitly in fact. But it was too soon. She was afraid that she'd make a fool of herself or say something she couldn't take back. He stole all thought from her when he was touching her. And he'd been touching her a lot more lately...

She sighed and looked out at the woods. They'd never gone this way before. He was taking the road toward Heller Mountain. She snuggled into his back and promised herself to keep her mouth shut about her feelings.

Bikers didn't care about love anyway. He might want her close at hand but she couldn't imagine him professing his love for her. Neither one of them were much for words. It was one of the reasons they were so well suited. Telling him that she loved him would only ruin things.

And right now, everything was perfect. Maybe he'd tell her what was bothering him tonight. But if he didn't, she wouldn't ask. She couldn't risk it.

****

Devlin pulled up the cabin after a leisurely 45 minute drive. He always went about 20 MPH slower when Kaylie was on the back of his bike. But even when he wasn't, he found himself being a bit more careful on the road. He had someone now. His devil may care attitude was shifting. He frowned, not sure he liked the change.

Devil's weren't supposed to be cautious. He shook off the feeling of foreboding that was coming over him. Tonight he would finally get what he wanted. He'd never waited for anything this long before in his life. His fingers itched to touch her skin as he parked and dismounted. Kaylie must have sensed his mood because she was quiet as he pulled off her helmet and led her to the front porch.

He fished around for the hidden key and unlocked the door. He flipped on a light and guided Kaylie inside. The cabin was rustic but clean. A frequent hide out for anyone in the SOS who needed to lie low, it had been in Dev's family since the 1950's. Other than that, his folks had brought him out here for vacations when he was kid. Now it was mostly unused.

She looked around her, taking it in.

"What is this place?"

"My Grandfather built it. Do you like it?"

She nodded her head but didn't say anything else. He could tell she was overwhelmed. Whether by the cabin itself, or the prospect of spending the night alone with him, he wasn't sure. He took her hand and pulled her to the back of the house.

"Come on, let me show you the best part."

There was a screen door that led to a back porch. He pushed it open and Kaylie made a sweet surprised gasp. The sun was setting over the small lake. It was unbelievably private. A tire swing hung on a tree branch, dangling over the water.

"It's beautiful!"

He smiled at the rapturous expression on her face.

"The view's even better from in here."

He took her back inside and up a flight of stairs into a large bedroom. He pulled her into his arms. He couldn't wait any longer. He needed her. He needed to forget the world and lose himself in her sweetness. She was looking down at his chest, looking very nervous suddenly. He licked his lips and lowered his head. He knew how to make her relax... how to drive her wild.

He took his time kissing her, using his mouth alone. After a while he pulled her closer to him, sliding his hands up and down her delicious back to cup her sweetly rounded bottom. When he pressed her against the hardness in his pants she sighed audibly. He groaned as he resisted the urge to grind himself into her softness. There was no need to rush. He'd told her mother she'd be home by dawn. They had all night. And he intended to use it.

****

Devlin was unbuttoning her blouse while he nibbled on her earlobes. Her sudden shyness was evaporating, just as the certainty that he was going to finally make love to her tonight was setting in. She had a general idea of the mechanics involved in sex, just none of the specifics. Thankfully Dev seemed to know exactly what he was doing.

Her breath was coming in little pants as he slid her blouse off and over her shoulders. He groaned as his hands closed over her thin cotton bra. He caressed her gently, kissing her mouth again before she felt him unhook her bra behind her. As soon as her bra was off everything changed. He stared down at her naked chest for a moment with an absorbed look on his face. Then he went wild. His hands were everywhere and his mouth- oh, his mouth was everywhere too. He lavished her breasts with attention endlessly before scooping her up and laying her on the bedspread. Then he pulled his shirt off and pressed himself against her.

Oh god-

The heat of his chest felt incredible against her breasts and stomach. He was kissing her again as he rocked his hips into hers. There was no doubt now. That's what he wanted to do.

She wanted to do it too.

She didn't protest when his fingers found the button on her denim shorts. He deftly undid them and pushed them down over her hips, taking her panties part of the way so that her body was barely covered at all. He leaned back and pulled her shorts off of her legs. Then he settled between her legs, slowly tracing his finger along the top edge of her panties while she waited breathlessly to see what he would do. He was staring at her junction with a heavy lidded look in his eyes. Heat radiated from his hands where they rested on her hips.

Finally he moved, one hand hovering over her mound. She shivered as he began lightly touching her through her panties, making small circles over her femininity before retreating. Then he began again, slowly teasing her until she was writhing on the bed. The weight of his legs pressed down on hers, holding her in place as her hips bucked slowly. Finally he leaned forward, kissing her as he used his other hand to pull her panties down and away.

Now his hand was on her bare skin, playing with the soft folds between her legs. She felt so warm down there... and surprisingly slick.

"Jesus Kaylie..."

She couldn't think straight as he brought her closer and closer to the edge, without letting her fall over it. Finally he pulled away and she watched as he pulled his jeans off and threw them aside. He was so beautiful... and big. Oh dear god, he was big.

Devlin's shaft stood straight up from his narrow hips, reaching nearly to his belly button. A small fearful gasp escaped her lips and he was back in an instant, kissing and soothing her.

"It's alright Kaylie. I promise."

She nodded but her body had gone stiff. The heat between her legs was still there but the rest of her was running for the hills, tensed up and prepared for pain.

"Shhhhh sweetheart, don't be afraid of me."

His soft words combined with his skillful hands started to relax her again as he slid his finger up and down the line between her nether lips. He wasn't pushing himself inside her or doing anything except kissing and touching her. Her body started to respond again, hovering on the edge of release.

"Oh!"

He suckled her nipples as his finger started to strum the tender nub above her opening. He slipped a slender finger inside her as she felt herself start to climax for the first time.

"Oh, oh, oh, OH!"

She hardly recognized the high pitched breathy sounds she was making as the world seemed to explode around her. Her body would have lifted off the bed entirely if he hadn't been lying partially on top of her. As she floated back to earth she felt him adjusting his weight as he positioned himself between her legs.

"Kaylie, look at me."

She opened her eyes with an effort and stared up at Devlin. The mysterious man she felt like she'd known forever. That she'd wanted forever... She nodded, giving him permission to move forward. She didn't care about the pain anymore.

She gasped with pleasure as he pushed the tip of his manhood against her opening. He was hard as a rock against her softness, but also silky... and incredibly hot. He pressed forward a few inches and just like that, he was inside her.

Ohhhh...

It felt good. Really good. He flexed his hips and the angle changed. She felt him slip deeper inside her. Her body felt stretched open and utterly exposed. But she knew he wouldn't hurt her. She watched his face as he eased himself out and back in slowly. His eyes were closed and it looked like he was concentrating with every fiber of his being. She realized he was struggling to hold onto his control. She wondered if it felt as good to him as it did to her.

He groaned as he rocked himself back into her again, a little deeper this time. It hurt a little bit now, but it was commingled with the most exquisite pleasure she'd ever experienced before, or even imagined. He fit inside her perfectly, filling her with liquid heat.

The pressure was starting to build inside her again as he worked himself in and out of her gently, gaining greater access with each stroke. Where was the pain she was supposed to be experiencing? Where-

Ouch!

He bumped up against something and they both moaned. Her barrier was preventing him from penetrating her fully. He held perfectly still above her.

"Kaylie."

"Yes?"

"I'm going to take you now."

"Oh... I thought you already were."

He let out a shout of strangled laughter.

"No, not quite yet."

"Okay."

"Listen- I'm going to try not to hurt you- I can squeeze by without tearing anything- but- hmmmfff- you're so tight that it's harder than I thought it would be-"

He moaned as she clenched down on him instinctively. Her hips were making tiny circles against him subconsciously. He closed his eyes tightly and pushed forward. She felt the membrane inside her give way. She'd always imagined he would just tear through it forcefully. From what she'd heard that was what was normal. But he'd done it so gently that he was embedded inside her without more than the slightest discomfort.

"Unffff... Jesus Kaylie you feel... so good... are you alright sweetheart?"

"Uh huh- yes- just- can you-"

He swallowed as he stared down into her big brown eyes. She looked so sweet and trusting- and so fucking hot that he could barely stop himself from plunging into her honied depths.

"Yes?"

"Can you, oh! Can you... move like you were before?"

Relief and desire poured through him. He hadn't imagined he could be more turned on than he already was, but he'd been wrong. Her sweet admission that she wanted him to get on with it made him want to laugh and lose himself inside her all at once.

"Yes, I can do that."

He pressed a kiss into her lips before letting his body take over. He kept himself in control, not going too fast but not too slow either. He could hardly believe she was finally his after all this time. Her body had exceeded his wildest imaginings, the way she looked and oh god- the way she felt. Even after he'd seen her in that bikini he hadn't expected her to feel this good... her skin was like silk. She was firm and smooth and rounded in all the right places. He didn't think he would ever be able to get enough of her.

He groaned and picked up the tempo. He could feel her responding to him. She was so natural and beautiful. Her body knew what to do and she let it happen without shame or embarrassment. She might be shy but that just added to her appeal. He grunted as he felt her squeeze down on him. There was no way he could last much longer.

Then he remembered that this wasn't a one time thing, that she was his old lady now and he could have her again, maybe even tonight if she wasn't too sore. He'd never had that feeling before- for the first time in his life he wanted more and he knew he would have it. The thought of having her again sent him over the edge. His hips jerked spasmodically, as he felt himself explode inside her. He filled her with his seed, pumping himself out of tempo as her body clenched down on him, pulling him deeper...

He lay on top of her, trying to catch his breath, unable to think or move for a moment.

Jesus.

He'd never come so hard in his life. Whatever power Kaylie had over him, whatever time he'd put in to make sure her mother wouldn't object, that he was free from encumbrances, that she would trust him, it had all been worth it. He knew nobody would ever make him feel this way again.

She was his.

****

Kaylie was laughing as she ran up to the house in her wet skivvies. It was freezing in the mountains. Who ever had decided it was a good idea to jump in the lake was insane! Actually, once she thought about it, she realized it had been her idea... more or less. He'd dared to her to do it after she'd asked him if he ever swam in the lake. They'd been lying in bed together... after...

The whole evening had been a blur. Making love. He'd held her for a long while afterwards. They'd had something to eat and then decided to skinny dip in the dark- well almost skinny dipping. She'd left her bra and panties on. She wasn't that comfortable with him yet! Besides, what if someone walked in on them?

She giggled and slammed the door behind her, pretending to lock Devlin out. He was buck naked, since he had not been wearing anything under his jeans. He'd mumbled something about going commando when she blushed and looked away. She wondered if he'd been naked all those other times they'd fooled around... the thought made her feel a little bit weak in the knees.

Dev appeared at the locked screen door, pretending that he was going to break it down. He snarled like a dog and then yipped at her when she opened the door. She was still laughing when he scooped her up and carried her back to the bedroom.

"How do you feel?"

She slid her arms around his neck. His muscled chest felt so warm. He looked so damn sexy!

"Good."

"Good?"

"Very, very good."

He brushed a strand of wet hair away from her face.

"I didn't hurt you?"

She blushed and looked away, peeking back up at him.

"Just a little. I thought it was going to be much worse."

He grinned and lifted her into his arms, depositing her on the bed.

"I did some research into this. The whole virgin thing is a fallacy. There's a membrane but it doesn't have to tear, you just need to nudge it out of the way."

She stared up at him while he grabbed a towel and started rubbing her down.

"You did that? For me?"

He grinned and tossed the towel aside, pouncing on her.

"Well, not just for you. I sort of enjoyed it too."

"Sort of!"

She squealed indignantly as he grabbed her and rolled her towards him.

"More than sort of."

He kissed her mouth.

"More than a lot."

He kissed her ear.

"More than ever."

He kissed her neck and she sighed, knowing he was going to make love to her again. Knowing she would love every second of it.

10

Dev was focused intently on the road as he drove Kaylie home in the early morning light. It had started to drizzle and he wanted to be extra careful. His earlier concern about losing his daring was gone. She was precious. She was his. He had to keep her safe. And he would.

She'd made him feel things that night that surprised the hell out of him. He'd known she was special. He hadn't know how special she would make *him* feel. He was changing already and he'd just started falling for her. He's wanted her for a long time but loving her, that was different.

Fucking *love* man.

He didn't even cringe back from the word now, not after she'd given him everything. And she had. She'd held nothing back when she was in his arms. Being with her was unlike anything he'd ever experienced. He finally understood why people believed in all the fairy tale bullshit he'd scorned for so long.

He was going to marry her.

Jesus!

He almost skidded out as the cop lights came on behind him. The blaring siren sounded like it was less than ten feet away. Where the hell had that come from? They must have been waiting in the woods for him to come down this way. But how would they know that? And why were they ambushing him?

He felt Kaylie hands tighten around his stomach as he pulled to the side of the road. This was not good. Not good at all.

He turned off the bike and spoke in a low tone over his shoulder.

"Don't say anything. I'll take care of this."

He looked back to see that there were two cop cars back there. Great. Office Grant and Sheriff Dooley were walking toward him with their night sticks swinging. Shit. He might have to take some licks this time. As long as they didn't touch her...

"If they hit me, just get out of the way."

"What? No!"

"Kaylie, just do it damn it!"

"What do we have here Officer Grant?"

The mocking drawl of Sheriff Dooley filled Devlin with dread. He'd never feared the police. Not until tonight. He forced a placid expression on his face.

"How can I help you Sheriff?"

"Who's that you got with you Dev?"

He cringed as Grant looked Kaylie over, grinning widely.

"My old lady."

"You don't say. Hey, aren't you the cutie who works down at Mae's?"

He didn't have turn his head to see Kaylie was afraid of Grant. He could just feel it. He tried to switch their focus off of the terrified girl behind him and back onto the matter at hand. It was hard to keep the scorn from his voice but he managed it.

"What seems to be the problem Sheriff?"

"We were looking for you."

"I'm flattered."

"Don't be. We have reason to suspect that you are involved in a felony. The attack of a young woman."

"What?"

"I said, you are being charged with attacking a young woman."

Grant slapped his thigh, still leering at Kaylie. Devlin felt like his stomach was falling into his boots.

"Oooeeee, she's a looker. Or she was until you roughed her up. Not like this one though. You sure have good taste for an outlaw."

"I haven't *attacked* anyone."

"Well, see, she says you did. And you being who you are, doesn't seem so far fetched. Criminal element and what not."

"When did she say this happened?"

"Last Saturday at the State Fair."

"He was with me."

The Sheriff leaned down and peered at Kaylie. Devlin gritted his teeth.

"What's that miss?"

"I said, he couldn't have attacked anyone because he was with me."

The Sheriff gave her an appraising look.

"All day and all night?"

"Yes."

"Well be that as it may, I'm going to have to take him in for questioning. Stand up now please Mr. McRae and face the bike."

Devlin closed his eyes and forced himself to comply. The bastards were doing this out of spite. It was just scare tactics. He hadn't attacked anyone and they knew it. He just wished they had picked a time when Kaylie wasn't with him. Never mind that they were in the middle of nowhere.

He felt the cuffs snap closed around his wrists and turned around, careful not to make any sudden movements.

"We'll bring you back for your bike *if* the charges are dropped."

"Somebody has to come pick up Kaylie."

Grant slapped his knee.

"Kaylie! That's it. I knew it. You sure look all grown up don't you now, darlin'?"

Sheriff Dooley pulled Devlin away just as Grant put his arm over her shoulders solicitously. He looked her over and grinned at Devlin.

"Don't worry about a thing Mr. McRae. I'll see the little darlin' home."

He felt rage boiling up inside him as he was pushed into the back of the squad car. If he hadn't of been cuffed he would have killed the man. He still might.

He watched as Kaylie followed the officer to the second car. She made eye contact with him through the window, trying to reassure him. She looked scared.

"I'll go to the club house! Don't worry!"

He gritted his teeth as Grant opened the passenger side door for Kaylie. At least he wasn't making her ride in the back. But if he touched her... he leaned his forehead against the padded wall separating him from the front and silently screamed.

They held him for three days. Three awful days during which Kaylie imagined horrible things happening to him. Her mind went wild, picturing every scenario in the book. All except Dev being guilty. That never even crossed her mind.

She'd been true to her word, getting her mother to drive her to the clubhouse as soon as that disgusting Officer Grant had pulled away. The way he'd looked at her... and spoken to her... it was revolting. He'd acted as if she was easy, a woman of ill repute. He'd even implied that he'd make sure Dev got out if she'd 'make nice' with him. She'd had to fight back the bile rising in her throat at his lurid insinuations. But he hadn't touched her.

She'd kept herself focused by thinking about Dev and what she would say when she got to the clubhouse. She'd never been there before but she knew where it was. Everyone in town did, mostly just so they could steer clear of the place.

The building had been cleaner than she'd expected. That is until she got to the bar room. There were people everywhere, bikers mostly but also a lot of women in various states of undress. There were two stripper poles in the room and each had a girl hanging off of them, dancing lazily. Everyone in the room was drunk except her.

Donnie had seen her immediately and been across the room in two seconds flat.

"You shouldn't be here. Dev wouldn't like it."

"He's been arrested- they said-"

He'd held up a finger, silencing her.

"Come on, let's find Jack. You can tell us both."

They'd pulled her into a hallway and waited until there was a break in the traffic to and from the bathrooms. Then she heard Jack say the first words she'd ever heard him say.

"What happened?"

She'd told them everything. Halfway through the story Donnie looked at Jack and said one word.

"Dani."

Jack had nodded and just like that, Donnie was gone. Kaylie had started crying then. The tension and worry had finally gotten to her. She leaned against Jack's shoulder and cried all over his leather while he held perfectly still.

11

They had nothing on him. He knew that. Dev sat in the dim light on the uncomfortable bench making plans. No one had come to see him, but he knew they'd tried. They'd taunted him with that information.

'Your little honey was here today. She looked so sad when we told her you couldn't come out and play.'

He clenched his fists and got into position to do another set of push ups. He didn't even know who had accused him and of what exactly. He had a strong suspicion it was Dani. If they tried to prove that he'd laid a hand on her... they'd have a hard time doing that. Any member of the SOS would come forward and take the fall for him. That's if Dani actually had any physical evidence. The Spawns had an attorney on retainer. He was coming by later today. He was almost as pissed off as Devlin was.

It was pretty clear the cops were using the trumped up charges against him to try and aggravate him into attacking a police officer. That was an old school technique. Now they were using every trick in the book to drag out his stay. He'd come close to taking the bait more than once. Officer Grant had an annoying habit of stopping by the dank cell they were keeping him in and dropping hints about what he'd done, and what he'd like to do, to Kaylie.

'I can't wait to take a big bite of that honey pie. Does she squeal when you stick her? I bet I can make her squeal. Almost did the other night too.'

Then Grant had started making squealing noises every time he walked by, the bastard. It almost worked. Instead Dev had used his famous self control to do deep inside himself, to imagine the kinds of things he would do to Officer Grant if even one word he'd said was true. And a few things he would do to him just for thinking them. Officer Grant's life was going to get very difficult from here on out. If he'd laid one finger on his woman though... he was in for the beating of a life time.

Violence was part of the MC life, but there was a time and a place for it. In this case he couldn't very well beat up an officer of the law, unless Grant didn't know for sure who was doing the beating. A bag over the head after a night out drinking was the easiest way. Hiring out was another. But Devlin wanted to be there. He wanted to hear the crunch when his fist connected with Grants big, fat mouth.

Simmering rage didn't come close to what he was feeling. The pot had long since boiled over and now he was just hot metal bouncing around on the stove.

Ready to burn someone.

****

Kaylie waited outside her house for her ride. Donnie had called her and said he was coming to pick her up, that Devlin was getting out. She felt elated momentarily before the worries started to set back in. She'd had a lot of time to think the past few days. She was starting to wonder if she'd let her heart get her into a situation she'd regret for the rest of her life.

She wasn't sure she was cut out to belong to a biker, let alone the President of the most notorious gang in Northern California. The thought of not being with him cut her deep inside. But the thought of being dragged through the mud over and over again was scaring the heck out of her. Even her mother was concerned, and she'd been firmly on Devlin's side since the beginning.

Donnie drove up in an SUV. She hadn't been expecting that. She climbed in and sat there nervously as Donnie turned off the radio and waited for her to put on her seatbelt. She'd dressed conservatively for the occasion in a simple navy dress with a pink cardigan and kitten heeled pumps. Her hair was down and she wore sunglasses. She didn't want Devlin to see the doubt in her eyes.

She knew the charges against him were false. He would never hurt a woman and he certainly wouldn't force himself on one. Why would he when every woman he came into contact with melted like butter? Including her.

Especially her.

The drive to the courthouse in the center of town seemed to last forever. And yet she was so nervous that she wished it took longer. Hours, not minutes. Days.

What would she say when she saw him?

****

Devlin stepped out into the sunlight. He'd finally been released on bail after hours of back and forth legal bullshit. His lawyer was still inside threatening to sue the department for harassment if they didn't drop the charges. He shielded his eyes. The bright light hurt his eyes after three days stuck in the dark cell. He was pretty sure they'd chosen the worst cell in the place. It sure didn't smell like it'd been cleaned in the last decade or so.

He inhaled deeply as he saw Kaylie climbing out of the SUV across the street. She turned toward the courthouse steps and saw him. They both froze. He took one step, and then another. Suddenly they were running toward each other and he swept her up into his arms.

She felt incredible. She smelled incredible. She was there for him after all. He hadn't been sure after everything that happened. He lifted his head to kiss her and tasted salt on her lips.

She was crying.

"Oh sweetheart don't cry. Please?"

She didn't say anything. She just nodded her beautiful head and continued the water works. Devlin put his arm around her shoulders and walked across the street to the SUV. He clapped Donnie on the back and climbed into the drivers seat.

"Where are we going?"

"They wouldn't drop the charges even though they're complete bullshit. You know that, right?"

"Yes. I went back in and told them you were with me again. They didn't listen."

"You didn't have to do that. But for now, I'm out on bail and I have to wear a monitor. They're coming to the clubhouse later to fit me with one."

She didn't say anything but Donnie leaned forward.

"It will be good to have you around all the time Dev. We missed you."

"Fill me in on what I missed when we get back. First thing I need is a shower."

"What's the second thing?"

Dev just grinned and glanced at Kaylie, leaving no doubt of what he meant. He wanted her.

"Okay man, what about the third?"

"Food. And a plan. We need to nip this shit in the bud."

"I hear that."

They pulled into the clubhouse parking lot and a stream of people poured out to greet him.

****

"You don't mind do you babe?"

Kaylie was enveloped in Dev's arms. They were finally alone in the small apartment above the club he used sometimes. It was just a bedroom with a small bathroom attached, but it was clean and had a place to sleep when he was at the club too late to go home. There were other bedrooms for rest of the Spawn throughout the clubhouse but this one was the most private and reserved for the President alone.

He was kissing her passionately for a while before he turned his head and rested his nose in her hair.

"Damn, you smell so good and I'm so filthy. I shouldn't be touching you."

"I don't mind."

She hadn't answered his first question about staying in the clubhouse. He didn't press her, thank goodness. She would have much rather visited with him at his house, or hers. It was true though that she didn't mind that he was dirty. It just felt so good to be in his arms again.

"Hmmmfff... oh god. Let me get washed up. I want to hold you."

She nodded and watched him strip down. He didn't just want to 'hold' her. That much was obvious. A thrill went through her as he exposed his body to her. He was pushing his jeans down over his washboard abs when he looked up and caught her staring. He grinned and stood proudly in front of her, his arousal already evident.

"Unless you want to join me?"

Kaylie shook her head breathlessly. She was already feeling overwhelmed and needed the time to get herself together. He sniffed himself and cringed.

"Yeah, I don't blame you. I'll be out in a flash."

Kaylie smiled as he disappeared into the bathroom. She looked around the room. He didn't keep much there. A few magazines and books. Clothes. A mini fridge. And of course, the bed... which she would be laying down on shortly. She felt butterflies fill her stomach as she looked at the bed. Would it be different this time? Now that she knew what to expect?

There was a mirror over a dresser and she walked over to it. She pulled off her sunglasses and put them aside, shaking out her hair. She stared into her eyes and tried to figure out what she was going to do... she knew what she wanted but she didn't know what she could handle... not yet.

There was only one way to find out.

Pictures were taped to the edges of the mirror. Johnny with a young Devlin and a pretty woman who must have been their mom. She traced the picture with her finger. He looked so young. But he already stood with bravado, clearly aware of his position as the man of the house. He couldn't have been older than sixteen and yet he looked utterly confident in every way. So young, but already a man. Already a protector.

It must have killed him that he couldn't save them.

She felt him behind her before she saw him. She closed her eyes as he pressed his body against her back, wrapping his arms around her waist. He kissed the crook of her neck as her head fell back onto his shoulder. Hot spirals of desire shot through her body. She knew that whatever her decision was, she would never have anything like this with anyone else. She opened her eyes and saw him staring at her in the reflection of the mirror. He was looking at her with a fierce look in his gaze. Affection, tenderness, possessiveness and something else...

Pure heat.

Her mouth opened in response to the look in his eyes. His hand slid up her body to cup her breast as he held her facing the mirror. He played with her nipples through her dress before letting his hand drop to the hem of her dress. She started panting as he lifted his hand up under her skirt to find her panties. Without breaking eye contact, he started to tease her, stroking the line of her cleft.

She could not have pulled her eyes from his even if her life had depended on it. She gave into the delicious feelings he was creating in her as he toyed with her femininity. He was clearly not in a hurry, despite everything he'd said before. Finally he pulled her panties down and started to explore her body in earnest. He released her waist and she leaned forward slightly, gripping the edge of the dresser for support.

She moaned as she felt him lift her skirt from behind and hold the tip of his cock at her entrance. He was staring down at the place where their bodies met but he glanced up at her before he pushed forward. He was making sure she was ready, that she wanted him. He was asking permission.

Whatever he saw on her face was more than enough. He grunted as the tip of his shaft slid inside her. He held her hips with both hands as he pressed forward. Watching him take her in the mirror was intoxicating. When she looked over at herself she almost didn't recognize the wanton woman being taken from behind. And loving it.

As soon as he was fully inside her everything changed. He dipped his hips and circled them, changing the pressure and angle without withdrawing. She would have fallen over at the sensation if he hadn't gripped her shoulder with one hand. His other hand slipped down and under her skirt again, toying with her jewel.

"Ohhhhh..."

He grinned at her reflection in the mirror as he worked her body with incredible skill, taking what he wanted but giving so much more. His finger picked up speed as he ground himself deep inside her, making her clench down on him without thought.

"Unfff... oh Kaylie... yes..."

She was whimpering like an animal as he brought her closer and closer until she finally tipped over the edge. Her body shook convulsively as he pumped himself into her with greater force now. She was gripping him unconsciously when she felt his shaft jerk inside her. Then he leaned forward over her, thrusting wildly as he unleashed himself against her womb.

He didn't stop moving until they were both spent. He kissed her neck tenderly before pulling himself from her body. He bent down and slowly pulled her panties back up from her ankles, smiling wickedly at her in the mirror. She closed her eyes as he adjusted her clothing back to normal. She opened her eyes and looked at herself. You would never know the proper young woman standing there had just rutted like an animal and loved every second of it.

Dev was pulling clean clothes on. She noticed he didn't bother with undershorts again. He grinned at her and sat on the bed, patting the spot beside him. She walked over and sat down.

"Are you hungry?"

"Not really."

He put his hand on hers and she got a terrible feeling that he was about to say something she didn't want to hear.

"Kaylie..."

"Yes?"

"Did Officer Grant mess with you- or touch you in any way?"

She looked at him, taken aback by the question.

"What do you mean?"

"I won't be angry sweetheart. Did he make you do anything?"

"No."

She looked away and crossed her arms over her chest, suddenly feeling ashamed. She'd done her best to put the whole thing out of her mind, and now he wanted her to revisit it? He put his hand on her back and stroked her soothingly.

"Kaylie? You can tell me. I gotta know sweetheart."

She took a deep breath.

"He didn't touch me. He just- looked at me."

She felt Devlin tense up beside her.

"What do you mean? Tell me exactly what happened Kaylie."

"He drove me home and he kept saying things about you- about how people call you sloppy seconds sometimes and he wanted to know if I knew what that meant."

Devlin cursed under his breath.

"Kaylie-"

Once the words started she couldn't stop them from pouring out.

"He told me what it meant. He said you had a different girl every night and the rest of the club took them when you got bored with them. He said he'd wait in line for sloppy seconds like me. He told me that I was damaged goods around here now that I'd been with you but that he wouldn't mind even if other guys did. He wanted to know if I'd been passed around the club yet."

Devlin's hand stopped stroking her back as she felt him clench his hand into a fist.

"Kaylie I swear to you that this is not like that. You are not like that. Not to me, or any-"

"And then- when we finally got back to town- to my street- he pulled over and he wouldn't- he wouldn't-"

His hand was back, holding her tightly around the waist, his head leaning into hers, resting it on hers, as if he was trying to absorb her pain.

"He wouldn't unlock the door. He just- looked at me. You know. At my chest. And- lower... He just sat there licking his lips and staring at me."

"He's a dead man."

She swallowed back tears. She hadn't told her mother or anyone what Grant had done. What he had implied that he could and *would* do. Soon.

"I'm so sorry baby. I promise you that will never happen again. He's gonna pay for that. In spades."

"No- please- I don't want you to get into trouble. I want you to be safe. Please Devlin!"

She turned into his arms and stared up at him entreatingly. He was furious. His jaw was locked and the look in his eyes would have been terrifying if it hadn't been anger on her behalf. She'd never seen him like this. But she had to make him promise her. She loved him. She couldn't let him do something stupid on her behalf.

She loved him.

"Promise me Devlin!"

He took a deep breath and nodded once, sharply.

"Good. Because I couldn't stand it if anything happened to you- because of me..."

She stood up and walked out of the room. Her pace quickened in the hallway until she was on the stairs, then running through the clubhouse to the street. She was out of the gate and a block away before he caught up- banging on the fence and calling her name. But he couldn't go after her. She'd known that when she ran.

****

Devlin was beside himself. He walked behind the club and found some old plywood to break. He kicked it until it cracked in half. Then he found another piece. This time he used his fists. After about twenty minutes he looked up and realized he had an audience. About twenty bikers and chicks were standing nearby watching him. He didn't blame them for staring. He never lost control like that.

"Grant. He's done."

Jack and Donnie looked at each other. Donnie cleared his throat.

"You want me to go to Mae's tonight?"

Devlin nodded. He could feel the pulse in his cheek from clenching his jaw so hard. His knuckles were bloody and raw but he didn't care about any of that.

What the hell was he going to do?

He felt sick at the thought of Grant treating Kaylie that way. Like she was a whore instead of his sweet angel. She hadn't wanted to tell him about it. She was trying to protect him he realized. Just the way he hadn't been able to protect *her*.

He walked back into the clubhouse and poured himself a shot of tequila. The first of many to come he decided. He started slowly but worked steadily toward oblivion. He was still sober when the technicians came to outfit him with an ankle bracelet. After they left though, all bets were off. He knew that Kaylie wouldn't be back tonight. He was starting to wonder if she'd be back at all.

Devlin stared straight forward as people clapped him on the back, congratulating him for getting out, saying he'd beat the rap, not to worry. He ignored them all, just stared straight ahead and imagined tearing Grant's head from his body.

He'd do it too. It didn't matter that he'd promised Kaylie he wouldn't. He'd messed with his woman. It was a point of honor now.

And a warning to anyone who ever considered messing with her again.

As if things couldn't get any worse, Dani chose that moment to walk into the clubhouse. She looked rough. It had been dark the night of the carnival so he hadn't noticed it, but she did look like she'd been beat up.

"Um, Dev? Can I talk to you for a second?"

He gave her a hard look. He was tired of her bullshit but she did look like she had something important to say.

He nodded curtly and turned back to his drink.

"Make it fast."

She stepped closer and lowered her head.

"The night of the carnival I talked to Grant. He said he wanted to put you away. I told him I would help him."

Devlin's head shot up from the bar.

"You what?"

"I know I shouldn't have but I was so mad at you. I wouldn't have actually done anything Dev, I swear."

He narrowed his eyes and stared at her. She did look contrite.

"Go on."

"When I asked him what he meant to do he said he was going to kill two birds with one stone. The first stone was getting himself laid. The second one was- getting you put away. For good."

He stared at her realizing what she was saying.

"He hurt you?"

She nodded.

"I'm almost glad he did. Because if I had turned on the club then I would have deserved it. But I didn't go through with it. He spared me that at least."

He stared at her, cursing under his breath.

"They wanted me to press charges against you Dev but I wouldn't. I'm so fucking sorry."

He nodded again and turned back to his drink.

"You are banned from the club."

She let out a tiny sob and turned away but he stopped her.

"Oh, and Dani?"

She turned back, fear and hope in her eyes.

"I'll make him pay for what he did to you. I promise you that."

She inhaled sharply and he saw a glimpse of the pretty girl he'd known so many years ago. She nodded, proudly this time and walked out of the club with her head held high.

12

Kaylie served a cheeseburger and turkey club to Mr. and Mrs. Marcus. They were a sweet old couple who came in at least once a week. Kaylie had always imagined she'd have something like that someday- growing old together, taking walks, raising a family.

But how could she ever have any of that with Dev?

Maybe he wasn't the problem. Maybe it was her. His lifestyle was extreme to be sure but he'd shown her that he was a good man time and again. Better than most she'd wager. So what if he rode a bike and hung out with a bunch of tattoo'd tough guys. They stuck together like glue. If any of them ever needed anything, Dev would be there for them and vise versa. They had loyalty and guts in spades. *Especially* Dev.

If she couldn't get past all of this then she knew she would be the one missing out. She had no doubt that Devlin would have another woman just by snapping his fingers. He might miss her, or even be really sad for a while, but she doubted he would experience the soul crushing loss that she was anticipating. Just thinking about being without him made her feel desolate and alone.

Maybe it was just better to turn a blind eye to the club and the troubles that went hand in hand with it. If the cops wanted to harass her, so be it. She would just toughen up. She loved Dev already. As time went on she was realizing that she wasn't even close to done falling for him. In fact, she couldn't think about anything else but him, and the way he'd made love to her that afternoon.

Her cheeks were flushed as she walked to Mae's to do her night shift. She had been glad for an excuse to get out of the club house. She'd needed time to think and she was almost certain she'd made her decision. Whether it was the right one or not was hard to say.

She tied her apron over her pink rayon uniform and got to work. It was busy tonight which was a blessing. It kept her mind off of... other things. Images of Dev and Grant were swapping places in her mind with intensely different results. She went from feeling very warm in the diner to wanting to run out back and upchuck all over her tennis shoes. So being busy was great. Until he walked in.

Officer Grant.

Her stomach felt like it dropped to her shoes. He was looking around the place as if he owned it. He caught sight of her behind the counter and his expression changed to one of unconcealed lust. He oozed his way toward the counter like the slime ball that he was and sat down in front of her.

He rested his big meaty hands on the formica counter. She had trouble looking away from them for a minute. Officer Grant was a huge man. Tall and strong but also getting close to thirty and starting to get fat. His hands looked pink and swollen laying there on the counter like two uncooked chicken cutlets. If he touched her with them she'd scream.

"Well, if it isn't my favorite little waitress. How are you doin' tonight honey?"

She flipped over her pad and stared at it, pen at the ready.

"What can I get you, Officer Grant?"

A disgusting smile crept over his face as he pondered the question. It was obvious that he was thinking about things that were *not* on the menu. And never would be!

"I don't know doll face. Do you have any specials tonight? Maybe a discount on something leftover, like sloppy seconds?"

She swallowed the bile rising in her throat. Was he kidding with that BS? Suddenly she started hoping that Dev would do something to the guy. Not kill him but... something bad.

Maybe she was cut out to be a biker's woman after all.

"Let me know when you're ready to order."

She slapped a menu down in front of him and walked away. She didn't see Donnie outside on his bike making a phone call.

****

Devlin was being held down by three guys. He'd taken the call from Donnie and ran out of the clubhouse before anyone could stop him. It was Jack who wrestled him off his bike to the pavement and then got a few other guys to help him hold Dev down.

Grant was at Mae's. Bothering Kaylie. Again.

His guts twisted at the thought of that pig talking dirty to his sweet girl. She'd lost her virginity less than a week ago and she was already dealing with this crap? It made his blood boil.

Enough so that he was ready to break the agreement of his release. If he left the clubhouse compound his ankle bracelet would go off and that would be it. Guaranteed jail time.

Then he wouldn't be able to protect Kaylie at all. Or touch her. Or...

He nodded curtly and the guys eased their weight off of him. He stood and brushed himself off then stalked back inside the club. He got up on a chair and put his boot on the bar.

"Listen up! We are having an outing. All of you are going to Mae's for banana splits."

A couple of the guys moaned amongst all the cheering.

"I'm lactose intolerant Dev!"

"Whatever- get what you want Lennie. The point is, that pig Grant is in there right now, messing with my old lady. I can't go anywhere. But you guys can."

In unison all the guys got up and ran for the door. The sound of 40 something hogs revving up and hitting the road was like music to his ears. He climbed down and reached behind the bar for a beer. Even the guy manning the bar had gone.

Grant was going to love this.

****

Mae's was full of leather. Kaylie stared around as she rushed to take everyone's orders. There were at least fifty bikers in the diner, all coming within the last few minutes. She saw Donnie and Jack had taken seats on either side of a suddenly nervous looking Grant.

She was worried about getting all the orders straight until she realized they were all getting the same thing. Banana split. Extra nuts. Well, all except for one guy who ordered sprite, mumbling under his breath 'food allergies.' She felt tears welling in her eyes. Dev couldn't have sent a clearer message to Grant. Or to her.

She was his. He would protect her.

Donnie was leaning in toward Grant and whispering something in an urgent manner. Jack said nothing as usual, but was following the conversation closely and nodding. When Kaylie brought Grant his check she looked him proudly in the face. Sloppy seconds didn't get this kind of escort home.

"Anything else Officer Grant?"

He shook his head and reached for his wallet. His hand was shaking slightly and his face was white as a sheet. Jack grabbed his hand, twisting it hard while Donnie grinned up at her and winked.

"No thank you. I'm- uh- sorry for not treating you like a lady."

She nodded at him regally.

"I accept your apology. Just see that it doesn't happen again. To any woman."

He nodded eagerly while his wrist was slowly wrenched underneath the counter.

"And tell Dev-"

She cocked an eyebrow at him.

"The charges are dropped."

With a whoosh of air he stood and dropped twenty bucks on the counter. In less than 30 seconds, he was gone.

A huge cheer went up from the crowd, bikers and staff alike. And then one of the prospects came behind the counter to help her dole out ice cream for everyone. He cleaned up afterwards too, much to Charlie's amusement. By the time they all left she had a stack of twenty dollar tips a couple of inches high.

****

He was waiting for her when she walked into the clubhouse. It was late. She'd finished her shift later than usual. There had been a lot of ice cream bowls to put away from what he'd heard. Jack had waited outside while Donnie went back to the club to pick up Dev's SUV.

There was a nervous knot in the pit of his stomach as she walked toward him through the crowd of bikers. They all smiled at her as she passed. She was one of them now. They loved her as much as he did.

Love. There it was again. No point fighting it now. He loved her, for better or worse. He was praying he wasn't about to get his heart ripped out by the woman he loved.

Finally she stood in front of him. She didn't smile or kiss him. She just raised her chin and stared him right in the eye.

"I didn't know if I wanted this kind of life."

His chest felt like it might explode but he forced his voice to remain steady.

"I understand. I won't be mad if this isn't what you want Kaylie. I could never be mad at you."

She looked down as if she were embarrassed about what she was saying. Like the words didn't come easy. He held his breath, hoping beyond hope that she wouldn't say they were through.

"I said I *didn't* know. But now I do."

When she looked up again he was shocked at the triumphant look blazing out of her eyes. It was strong and sure and confident. It was full of love. For him.

"I'm yours Devlin. For as long as you want me."

He almost laughed but he felt emotion choking his throat, making it tough to even talk. He cupped her face and stared into her eyes.

"Forever Kaylie. Is that long enough?"

She nodded as he watched tears fill her beautiful eyes. He clasped her to him harder and bent his lips to hers.

"Forever."

We hope you enjoyed *Wanted By The Devil!* Joanna is already hard at work on the next book in the *Devil's Riders* series, also a collaboration with Pincushion Press, an independent publishing house with a focus on romance.

Joanna loves to hear from her fans! Please contact her at JoannaBlakeRomance@gmail.com

You can also follow her on her blog and twitter!

http://jbromancenovels.tumblr.com/

https://twitter.com/JBromancenovels

Printed in Great Britain
by Amazon.co.uk, Ltd.,
Marston Gate.